TILLY'S PONY TAILS

Parkview Pickle

the naughty show pony

TILLY'S PONY TAILS

Parkview Pickle
the naughty show pony

PIPPA FUNNELL

Illustrated by Jennifer Miles

Orion
Children's Books

First published in Great Britain in 2010
by Orion Children's Books
a division of the Orion Publishing Group Ltd
Orion House
5 Upper St Martin's Lane
London WC2H 9EA
An Hachette UK Company

1 3 5 7 9 8 6 4 2

A catalogue record for this book is available from the British Library.

ISBN 978 1 4440 0083 2

Printed and bound in the UK by CPI Mackays, Chatham, ME5 8TD

www.orionbooks.co.uk
www.tillysponytails.co.uk

For George Nolan, my newly-arrived
nephew, named after my father

One

A normal day for Tilly Redbrow involved getting up early to feed, muck out and groom her favourite horse, Magic Spirit, before taking him for a morning ride across the fields. When she got back there was usually time for a slice of toast in the Silver Shoe Farm club room, then it was off to school.

After school, Tilly was back at Silver Shoe.

She would help Angela, the owner,
with whatever needed doing. This
could be exercising the other horses,
sweeping the yard, or sorting out
some old tack. Tilly didn't mind
as long as it was pony-related.
Then there was more feeding
and grooming, and perhaps
a lesson if she was lucky. At
the end of the day, Tilly always
enjoyed spending some quiet time with
Magic and saying goodnight. After Silver
Shoe, there was homework and tea, and
by seven o'clock she was exhausted, but
it was worth it to do what she loved.

Tilly had loved horses for as long as
she could remember. She'd read countless
copies of *Pony* magazine and played dozens
of pony-themed computer games, but it
wasn't until she'd got involved
with Silver Shoe Farm
that she'd experienced
the real thing. And the
real thing was great.

'I can't wait to find out more,' said Mia,
as she and Tilly sat outside the tack room,
rubbing soap into their saddles. It was a
mild early autumn evening and the sun was
beginning to set. They were talking about
the horsehair bracelets that Tilly and her
brother, Brook, wore. They'd both been
given them as babies, before they were
adopted.

'Apparently there's a Native American tribe who wear horsehair bracelets because horses are such an important part of their lives,' said Tilly. 'The owner of Tregenny Farm, where Brook and I went on holiday, told us about it. We looked it up on the internet. We don't know whether there's a connection between their bracelets and ours yet – but we're going to try and find out.'

'It would be cool if there is.'

'Definitely.'

'I wish something exciting like that would happen to me,' said Mia, sighing. 'I can't even find a new horse. I'm fed up of borrowing rides from different people. It's just not the same.'

It had been a while since Mia had grown out of her pony, Rosie. Luckily, Rosie was being kept on at Silver Shoe to help other children, but Mia had yet to get a horse of her own.

'My parents say I'm being too fussy,' she said. 'But they don't seem to understand. I don't want any old horse. I want the right horse. I want to have that special bond, like you and Magic.'

'I understand,' said Tilly. She knew all about special bonds. She wouldn't swap Magic for anything.

Tilly smiled. Then she looked up and saw Angela coming towards them.

'Hi, girls.'

'Hi, Angela.'

Angela was holding a plan of the stable yard and looking a bit confused.

'I'm just trying to work out where I'm going to fit all the horses. This is the busiest Silver Shoe's ever been, what with all the thoroughbreds we've been bringing on, and we've got a new pony arriving tomorrow.'

'Who's that?' asked Tilly.

'Her name's Parkview Pickle, Pickle for short. She belongs to a girl called Cynthia, who's very into showing. Takes it really seriously. I met her and her mum last week, and her mum's already given me a

long list of dos and don'ts. I hope Pickle
isn't as fussy.'

'Where are you putting her?'

'I thought one of the quieter areas near
Magic Spirit would be good. Maybe you

two could help settle Pickle and Cynthia in?'

Tilly and Mia nodded.

'Great. I'd like both of you to get more involved in helping me around the riding school this year. You're good role models for the younger students. You can show them the ropes and encourage them to be responsible around the yard. Maybe help out with a few riding lessons. Make sure they clean their tack and keep the place tidy, that sort of thing. Hopefully then they'll all become as hard-working and committed as you. Is that okay?'

'Sure,' said Tilly.

It was better than okay. It was an honour.

When Angela had gone, Tilly and Mia looked down at their saddles. They'd been cleaning them for twenty minutes and were about to give up.

'Let's give these another going over,' said Mia. 'I want mine to be perfect.'

'Me too.'

They set to work again, polishing. Angela's words, it seemed, were highly motivating.

Two

Next day, Tilly was eager to get to Silver
Shoe to greet Parkview Pickle and Cynthia,
who were arriving at ten. It was also a
Saturday, which meant all day with the
horses, so she wanted to make the most
of it. Her mum gave her a lift, dropping her
off on her way to North Cosford market.
Tilly went straight to Magic's stable to
muck out and give him his morning feed.

'Hello, boy,' she said softly, as she
entered, so as not to startle him.

Magic came directly to her and began nuzzling her shoulder. She slipped him a carrot, which was one of his favourite treats.

'You'll have a new neighbour joining you today,' she explained. 'I want you to be very friendly and welcoming. Angela says we're role models now, so we've got to be on our best behaviour.'

Magic looked at her. He seemed to be listening, but Tilly recognised a cheeky twinkle in his eye that said, 'I'm Magic Spirit, I'll be good if I want to!'

'Okay, okay,' she said, sensing Magic's independent streak. 'As long as you're nice to the new pony at least.'

Over time, Magic had developed a reputation for being a bit temperamental. With Tilly, he was a dream horse, always cooperative, always calm. But whenever other people tried to do things with him, including experienced handlers like Duncan, Silver Shoe's head boy, he became restless.

Angela's father, Jack Fisher, said it was a 'favouritism' thing. And even though it meant hard work for other people, Tilly was glad to be Magic's favourite. He, after all, was her favourite. Around the stables, everyone knew, if something needed to be done with Magic, Tilly was the person to call.

'Let's get you ready,' she said, leading him into the yard. 'How about stretching your legs along the country lanes? Just a quick ride this morning, so we can be back in time to see Parkview Pickle.'

Magic nodded his head and snorted.

It wasn't long before he was brushed and tacked up. Tilly usually liked to take her time doing these things, but when she had to get going, she could be very quick. After all, she was well-practised!

It was a peaceful morning as they began to trot along the familiar network of farm tracks and lanes. The air was fresh and the grass was still dewy. They headed for the small hill that overlooked North Cosford. As they went, Tilly wondered what new arrival, Pickle, and her owner would be like. Friendly, she hoped. And fun. Although the mum sounded quite demanding – maybe Cynthia wouldn't be the same.

At the top of the hill, Tilly and Magic paused for a while. Tilly loved the feeling of being very tall, up on Magic's back, looking down on the world. She felt as though she was in an old-fashioned Western movie, staring across the desert. It made her think of her birth mum and the

Native American tribe. She was certain this
tribe could be the key to finding out more.
She couldn't quite explain why. It was
just an instinct. The next step was for her
and Brook to find a way of contacting the
tribe and asking some questions. That way,
they'd know for sure.

She gave a deep, contented sigh. Then
she nudged her heels, signalling Magic to

walk on. When they reached the bottom of the hill, and hit the flat, they moved into a canter.

'Back to Silver Shoe, boy. Let's pick up the pace.'

Ten minutes later, they were back at the stables, but there was no sign of Parkview Pickle or her owners. Tilly dismounted and met Mia in the yard.

'I'm thirsty,' said Mia. 'I've got a mouth full of dust. I've been helping Duncan unload a delivery of hay. Let's go and make some lemonade.'

'Mmm. Good idea. Then we can watch for Pickle's arrival.'

Tilly tied Magic up, and followed Mia to the club room.

'I hope Cynthia's nice,' said Tilly. 'Especially if we're going to be helping her settle in.'

Mia crushed lemon halves into a jug and swirled in some sugar. She added water and ice, then a bit more sugar. As she began pouring the lemonade into glasses, the sound of an engine drifted through the open window.

'That sounds like a horsebox,' said Tilly.

The girls abandoned the lemonade, climbed on to the sofas and pressed their faces to the window.

'The horsebox of horseboxes!'

Outside, a large vehicle was reversing into position. It was brand new, one of the latest designs. It looked very impressive.

'How lucky is Pickle to get to ride around in that?!' gasped Mia.

A confused, dark brown pony emerged from the box. She wasn't very tall, but she had a chunky stature, which didn't seem to match her beautifully sloping neck and small, dainty face.

She was being led, or rather, pulled, by a woman wearing top-of-the-range riding gear. Halfway down the ramp, the pony

stopped and stamped her hooves.
The thumps reverberated around
the yard. Duncan and a couple of
others came over to help, but it was
clear the pony didn't want to do as
she was told.

Finally, after several attempts
and lots of struggling, the pony
stepped down on to the concrete.
She sniffed the Silver Shoe Farm
air, then lifted her head and shook
out her mane, as if to say, 'I've
arrived!'

'I guess that must be Parkview
Pickle,' said Tilly. 'Pickle by name,
pickle by nature!'

'Uh oh,' said Mia. 'If you think
she's trouble, listen to her owners!'

From behind the horsebox,
came Cynthia. She was moaning
loudly at the woman holding Pickle
about the reason they were late.
Neither of them seemed to care
that everyone was watching.

'It's your fault!' said Cynthia.

'Why is it my fault?'

'I told you not to go on the motorway. You never listen to me.'

'And I told you not to tell me what to do!' said Cynthia's mum.

Mia gulped.

'What have we taken on?'

Three

Tilly and Mia went straight out to the
yard to greet the new arrivals. Luckily the
arguing had stopped by now. Cynthia
stood beside Pickle feeding her mints,
while her mum talked to Angela. Cynthia
was like a mini version of her mum,
thought Tilly. They both had perfect
brunette curls, green eyes, and dimples
on their chins.

Tilly knew she had to be friendly, even
if Cynthia did seem a bit stroppy. She

remembered how the Silver Shoe gang had
welcomed her on her first day. Back then,
she'd never even ridden a horse before,
but everyone had been lovely and made
her feel as though she belonged.

'Hi. You must be Cynthia,' she said,
in her friendliest voice. 'I'm Tiger Lily,
Tilly for short, and this is my friend, Mia.
Has she had a good trip?'

Tilly gestured towards Pickle and gently patted her shoulder. Talking about ponies was always a good place to start.

'Oh, she's been fine,' said Cynthia. 'She's used to travelling with all the shows we go to. This was no distance, compared to some of the journeys we've done.'

'Do you show her a lot then?' asked Mia

'Most weekends,' said Cynthia, shrugging. 'You love it don't you, Pickle-Wickle?'

Cynthia leaned towards Pickle and offered her another handful of mints. Pickle munched them, then Tilly noticed her side-step, as if to say 'leave me alone'. Something definitely wasn't right, she thought. Pickle had an attractive face and a beautiful dark brown coat, but she didn't have the lean physical condition of a busy show pony. And though she took the treats Cynthia gave her, she didn't seem to want to be near Cynthia herself.

'Do you win much?' said Mia.

'I used to on my old pony, Mr King. We used to win everything. We won the Tiny Tots Lead Rein at the Winter Championships when I was seven, and we won lots of sashes in the First Ridden Pony class. Then I got too tall, so my mum bought me Pickle. We're aiming for Supreme Champion at every show in the south and one day we're going to be big

stars at Horse of the Year. My mum says
we're the best.'

Mia rolled her eyes, but Tilly was
careful not to show any reaction. She was
more concerned about Pickle. She stroked
the pony's mane.

'Horse of the Year, eh? Good for you,
Pickle.'

She tickled Pickle's nose and let her
sniff the horsehair bracelets dangling
around her wrist.

'There you go, girl,' she said quietly.

As she said this, Pickle's eyes met hers.
They gazed at each other for a few seconds.

Tilly could see something in Pickle's expression – a sort of weariness – which made her think Pickle was a little less bothered about winning Horse of the Year than her owner. Tilly knew it wasn't the right time to mention this to Cynthia, but she also knew this was a pony that needed help.

'Oh well,' she said, smiling at the others. 'Let's get Pickle some water. She must be thirsty. Then we'll give you a tour of the stables.'

After showing Cynthia around the yard, Tilly and Mia took her down to the long field and grazing pastures. As they walked, Cynthia discussed Pickle's daily routine. It sounded pretty intense.

'We practise our paces every day from seven till eight. Then Mum drives me to school – except in the week before an important show, when I get days off for extra practice.'

Tilly and Mia glanced at each other. They wished they could get days off school to spend time at Silver Shoe, but there was no way they'd be allowed. They had to fit their riding around their education, and

secretly, they knew it was probably good for them.

'While I'm at school, providing it's a nice day, Pickle goes out in the field, but she's not allowed near other horses in case they have bad manners. We don't want her picking any up.'

'Looks like she's got a few of those already,' whispered Mia.

Tilly frowned. Poor Pickle. It seemed as though every bit of her life was geared towards being on her best behaviour at shows. She had no chance to just be a pony. Pamper, pamper, pamper. Everything was controlled. Tilly knew training was important but so, too, was fun. She kept her thoughts to herself though. She wanted to find out more before she got on the wrong side of Cynthia.

'So what made you come to Silver Shoe?' she asked.

'Our old farrier recommended this place. He said Angela and Duncan have a great reputation. We've just moved to a

cottage in Little Renton, which isn't that
near, but Pickle needs to have the best,
so it's worth the journey – at least I hope
it will be.'

'It'll definitely be worth it,' said Mia.

'Our next show is the Cosford County
Fair next weekend,' said Cynthia. 'My
mum says we've got to make a big impact
on the judges there because they do a lot
of the big shows in the south. It's very
important.'

'We'll help you get ready for that, if
you like,' said Tilly, keen to make an effort
for Pickle's sake. 'Mia has lots of tricks for
getting better paces out of the ponies she
rides.'

'And Tilly's a natural. If you've got a
pony problem, she'll know how to solve it!'

'Thank you,' said Cynthia. 'But I rarely
have problems. I've trained with the best
and Pickle has top show pony bloodlines
so she's hardly going to need help.'

'Suit yourself,' said Mia, with a small
shrug. 'Shall we go and finish the rest

of that lemonade? When the weather's nice, it's a Silver Shoe tradition to drink homemade lemonade in the club room.'

'Is it organic?' asked Cynthia. 'My mum only wants me to eat organic food. And I'm not supposed to have sugar in case I put on too much weight and can't fit into my best jodhpurs and navy jacket.'

Tilly and Mia looked at each other. Cynthia was going to be quite a challenge.

Four

The following morning, Tilly was up
extra early to feed Magic. She was excited
because she and Mia were riding over to
Cavendish Hall boarding school to join
her brother, Brook, and their friend, Cally,
for an early morning ride.

When she got to the yard, she noticed
Pickle looking out of her stable. Despite
being in a hurry, Tilly went over to greet
her. She was keen to see what Pickle
was like without Cynthia around. She

remembered what Jack Fisher told her
about good horsemanship: don't be
impatient with horses, act as if you have all
the time in the world.

'Hello, young lady. Did you have a good
first night? I hope you like it here at Silver
Shoe. I've been hearing all about your
showing and training. Sounds . . . intense.
No offence, but I would have thought,
with all that activity, you'd be a skinny
little thing. But you look more like you're
bordering on obese! Are you getting a bit
too much food?'

Pickle stared at Tilly with her big
eyes and long lashes and gave a little
whinny. Tilly could tell it was the noise
of an anxious pony, rather than a happy,
confident one.

'It's okay, girl,' she said gently, reaching
towards her.

As soon as Tilly's hand touched Pickle's
muzzle, the little pony relaxed. She
lowered her head and allowed Tilly to run
her hand beneath her neck and over her

shoulders. The affection seemed to soothe her.

'That's it,' said Tilly. 'You relax, girl. You need to start enjoying life.'

Suddenly, the sound of a car engine in the lane distracted them. Another early arrival. It was a neat, sleek sports car. Cynthia stepped out of the passenger door, dressed in smart jodhpurs and expensive-looking boots. Her mum kissed her goodbye and reminded her to train hard. Cynthia marched into the yard, trying to look awake and alert, although Tilly could see the tiredness in her eyes.

'Good morning,' said Tilly. 'I was just saying hi to Pickle. She seems to be settling well.'

'That's good,' said Cynthia, yawning. 'Because we've got work to do. Hello, Pickle-Wickle. I've got your favourite – marshmallows!'

Tilly stared at the bumper bag of sweets in Cynthia's hand. She was horrified at the idea Pickle might be snacking on them.

'Do you always give her these?'

'She loves them.'

'For breakfast?'

'Everyone deserves a treat occasionally, don't they, Pickle-Wickle? '

Cynthia cuddled up to Pickle and waved the marshmallows in front her. Pickle sniffed them then side-stepped a little, just as she had done the day before.

'That's pretty,' said Tilly, noticing a bridle with a glittery brow-band on top of Cynthia's bag.

'This is what she'll be wearing to the county fair,' Cynthia explained. 'And I'll wear my hair in bunches with ribbons to match it.'

As Cynthia got on with her routine, so did Tilly. She greeted and kissed Magic, then led him into the yard. She began forking his bedding, although she couldn't help keeping a watchful eye on Cynthia and Pickle. Pickle was clearly unhappy and, maybe she was being too quick to judge,

but Tilly was sure Cynthia had something to do with it. It would be interesting to see how they performed together.

Once Magic was tacked up, Tilly put on her riding hat and mounted. She met Mia and Red Admiral in the yard. Mia was borrowing Red for the morning, which was quite a treat because he was such an elegant, graceful horse. It was a fifteen minute steady walk to the gates of Cavendish Hall, and because Tilly had spent a while catching up with Cynthia and Pickle, they were running late. It didn't matter though. Brook and Cally would wait for them.

The roads were quiet as they began their journey. Only a few cars passed them. On a week day the same roads were usually busy with people driving to work. Tilly was always slightly nervous when riding on the roads in case any cars came along too fast. Or she worried that a bird might startle the horses, and make them spook into the path of a passing car. Tilly knew it was important to be sensible and keep her wits about her when she was riding on the roads, and she tried to remember what Angela had told her: 'Don't be afraid to use hand signals to slow the traffic down, and nod your head or raise a hand to say thank you. And if a large lorry comes along, make the driver wait, then trot on to the nearest gateway or driveway so that he can pass.'

There was a lot to think about, but even so, Tilly was glad to be on horseback. After she left school, she wanted to own a livery yard, like Angela, and never have to wear stuffy suits or make her way to an office every day. She and Brook had talked about running a riding centre by the sea.

Brook was a big part of Tilly's life now, but before she'd come to Silver Shoe Farm, she hadn't known he existed. And she hadn't realised he was her brother until she'd discovered he wore an unusual horsehair bracelet, just like hers. It was no coincidence, she thought, that she and Brook loved horses. She hoped that Native American tribe would answer some of their questions.

As Tilly and Mia turned the corner, alongside the leafy rhododendron bushes, they saw the familiar outline of Brook's black thoroughbred, Solo. Brook was standing beside him, chatting to Cally, who was holding her horse, Mr Fudge.

'Hi, guys,' Tilly called.

They waved.

'Sorry we're late. We've got a new pony at Silver Shoe and she's being a bit of a . . . pickle!'

Tilly told them all about Cynthia and her show pony ambitions, about the bag of marshmallows and about Pickle's unhappy manner.

'Marshmallows?' said Brook, horrified. 'They can't be good for a little pony.'

'Not such a little pony,' said Mia. 'She's like a plump pudding.'

'Sounds like a challenge for Silver Shoe's number one horse whisperer,' said Brook.

'Maybe,' said Tilly, twiddling her horsehair bracelet, and wondering what she could do to help.

The four friends rode side by side across the fields, then took a muddy bridle path. The hedgerows were dotted with ripe blackberries. The air was fresh and the sound of birds singing echoed through the trees.

'I found out some more stuff about Native American tribes,' said Brook.

'What?' said Tilly excitedly.

'Well, there are loads and they all have different customs and traditions. But I did find a few new details about the one Lillian at Tregenny Farm mentioned; the ones who wear the horsehair bracelets. They've mostly moved to the cities now, but there

are a few still left, carrying on with their traditional way of life. They live on a small reserve in Colorado. They've watched over free-roaming Mustangs on the plains for centuries, and they're believed to be some of the most skilled horsemen around.'

'Wow,' said Mia. 'Do you think you could be descended from them?'

Tilly didn't answer. She was lost in

a vision of herself and Magic galloping among a herd of wild Mustangs. It was so vivid, she thought she could almost feel the heat of the desert, the thud of ground beneath Magic's hooves.

'What do you reckon?' said Brook, bringing her back to reality. 'Could we be related? It's possible. In the photos we have of our mum she's wearing Native American clothes.

45

And the horse in the photo definitely looks like a Mustang.'

'It would explain a lot about you two, and your talent for looking after horses!' said Cally.

'But our mum doesn't look very Native American,' said Tilly. 'Maybe she was just on holiday?'

'She may not look very Native American,' said Cally, 'but how many times have people said you look like Pocahontas, Tilly?'

This was true. Tilly had always assumed it was because of the way she wore her hair, in two long plaits, but she also had an olive complexion. So did Brook.

'Well, maybe your mum's from England,' Cally suggested, 'but your dad might belong to this tribe!'

Tilly caught Brook's eye. It was a thrilling thought. Magic shook his mane and snorted. He obviously thought so too.

Five

Tilly and Mia returned to Silver Shoe just as the yard was getting busy. Mia had to rush off because she was going to spend the day looking at horses.

Tilly said goodbye to Mia and wished her luck then, having groomed Magic off, she led him out for a pick of grass, thinking they might see what Cynthia was up to.

'I wonder if Cynthia and Pickle are still training?' she said. Magic gave her a curious look. 'I want to see how well Pickle goes.'

Tilly led Magic round to the sand arena. Sure enough, Cynthia and Pickle were there, with a weary-looking Duncan, working on their paces. By the look on everyone's faces, things were not going well. Every time Cynthia asked Pickle to do something, the pony lowered her head, swished her tail and moved more slowly, her ears flat back. Tilly could hear Cynthia whining.

'Why is she doing this? It's not fair.
She's supposed to be a top show pony.
None of the other top ponies do this. We're
showing next weekend. At this rate, we'll
be nowhere near ready!'

When Duncan spotted Tilly at the fence, he came over.

'Having some Pickle problems?' said Tilly.

'Cynthia problems more like,' said Duncan, exasperated. 'A little show pony doesn't need the same level of training as a top dressage horse. I've tried to tell Cynthia, but she won't listen. She just wants to keep working. Pickle's had enough. All this non-stop training is counterproductive.'

Tilly could tell Duncan was really wound up. It wasn't like him to be so critical.

'Pickle looks frustrated,' she said. 'Ignoring aids – it's as if she's trying to tell Cynthia to give her a break.'

'Exactly,' said Duncan. 'Her behaviour is the only way she can communicate her feelings.'

'I think she needs the chance to be free,' said Tilly thoughtfully. 'I've been watching Cynthia and Pickle together since

they arrived. Every second of the day is
timetabled around preparing for shows. But
maybe Pickle needs time to just be a pony,
you know, hang out with the other horses
at Silver Shoe and play.'

'Absolutely,' said Duncan. 'That's
why you get on so well with horses, Tilly.
You've got a natural instinct for how to get
the best from them. No amount of training
will make a horse successful if their owner
doesn't understand their needs.'

'Does a marshmallow breakfast count
as ignoring a horse's needs?'

'If that's what the horse is having
instead of nutritious food, then yes. Why
do you ask?'

'From what I've seen . . . ' said Tilly
cautiously. She
didn't want to
be a tell-tale,
but she knew
Pickle's health
was at stake.
' . . . I don't think

Pickle has a very balanced diet. Cynthia gives her lots of snacks and treats. She gets

quite a lot of hay too, as well as a full bucket of hard feed.'

'Which explains why she's so heavy,' said Duncan. 'It's a good job you mentioned it, Tilly. Over-feeding is all too common a problem. Owners think they're giving their ponies love by indulging them with extra food, but what they're actually doing is helping them to become overweight and unhealthy. It puts much more pressure on their limbs, and more fat around their vital organs. Sounds like Cynthia could do with some feeding advice.'

'Duncan!' Cynthia's voice pierced the air.  'You're supposed to be helping me!'

'I think that's enough training for today,' Duncan called. 'Why don't you

finish there and take Pickle in, then we'll
have a chat about a few things?'

'But we haven't finished yet! We need
to practise standing and trotting up.'

As Cynthia said this, Pickle made a
beeline for the fence, squashing Cynthia's
legs against it.

'Ow! Stop it!' she yelled.

Tilly watched. Cynthia didn't use
any aids to stop Pickle. She just shouted.
Although Tilly was worried about Cynthia's
safety, she also felt sorry for Pickle. It was
clear she was trying to tell Cynthia she'd
had enough. Duncan ran over to them and
led Pickle away from the fence.

'That's enough,' he said again,
practically lifting Cynthia out of the saddle
and on to the ground.

Tilly noticed Pickle moved away
from Cynthia as quickly as she could, and
approached Tilly and Magic. Cynthia
folded her arms and frowned. She looked
as though she might stamp her feet.

'How are we going to win at the

Cosford County Fair if we're not allowed to train!?' she yelled at Duncan. 'I'm telling my mum!'

Tilly couldn't believe Cynthia's tantrum. She worried that the shouting would distress Magic and Pickle, but luckily they seemed too interested in each other to notice. It was lovely to see, especially because Magic could sometimes be anxious around other horses. His troubled past had made him very sensitive.

With Pickle it was different. Magic stood over her protectively, as though he wanted to look after her. They sniffed at each other's noses. Tilly thought Pickle looked glad to be in the company of another horse, with nothing expected of her.

Later that day, Angela caught up with Tilly in the yard.

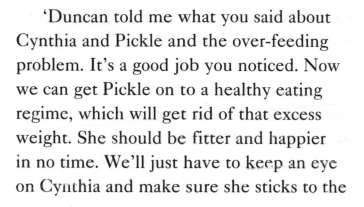

'Duncan told me what you said about Cynthia and Pickle and the over-feeding problem. It's a good job you noticed. Now we can get Pickle on to a healthy eating regime, which will get rid of that excess weight. She should be fitter and happier in no time. We'll just have to keep an eye on Cynthia and make sure she sticks to the

diet. No sneaky treats. Horses simply don't need them.'

'I'll keep a look out.'

'Great, and maybe you could give Cynthia some tips on general pony care, help her to get on better with Pickle. It might be nicer coming from you, since you're the same age.'

'Sure.'

'Oh, and Cynthia's mum phoned and left a message. She said something about Cynthia being 'too upset' to ride, groom and feed Pickle this evening. I agreed to make an exception this once. Is there any chance you could . . . ?'

'No problem,' said Tilly.

'Thanks. You're a life-saver!'

With that, Angela rushed off. Tilly didn't mind the extra work. She loved the fact that Angela trusted her and thought her responsible enough. And besides, this had given her an idea.

She grabbed Pickle's grooming kit from the tack room and headed straight for her stable.

'Hey, you,' she said. 'I'll be looking after you this evening. I'm going to take you down to the paddock. You can go out with Magic for an hour. You two can have some time together. But I'm afraid this is the one field we have with very little grass in it – sorry!'

She brushed Pickle down and combed her tail. As she did this, she collected the loose hairs and put them in her pocket. She'd decided to make a bracelet for Cynthia. Cynthia had some spoilt-brat ways, but Tilly still wanted to get on with her, at least so she could help Pickle.

Tilly led Pickle to the field and watched as the little pony went towards Magic. It was like watching two old friends get together for a gossip.

'Just relax, Pickle. There'll be no training tonight. And as for you, Magic,' she said, catching his eye. 'You obviously listened when I asked you to make Pickle feel welcome. Good boy.'

Six

That evening, at home, Tilly worked
through her collection of *Pony* magazines
to see what helpful tips she could find for
Cynthia and Pickle. She'd been meaning
to do this since they arrived at Silver Shoe
but there just hadn't been time. Tilly noted
any useful things down on her horse-shaped
notepaper and called them 'Cynthia's Tips
for the Top'. Then, after tea, she went
online and found one of her favourite pony
chat forums. She posted a question.

How do I help a naughty show pony get on better with her rider? Rider is v. fussy and wants things to be perfect. Pony refuses to listen or pushes her into fences. Advice please.
TillyMagic

Tilly waited. She finished her homework, played a few rounds of Stable

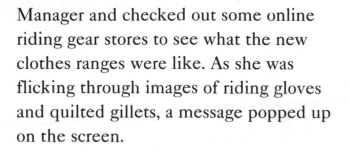

Manager and checked out some online riding gear stores to see what the new clothes ranges were like. As she was flicking through images of riding gloves and quilted gillets, a message popped up on the screen.

Sounds like the pony needs more play-time. Get pony and rider to have fun together in the paddock, going through bending poles or playing gymkhana games. Need to rebuild the relationship between them, so lots of time spent handling on the ground, grooming, etc. Hope this helps. Ponyswift89

Tilly was pleased. This confirmed what she'd thought all along. Pickle was getting bored and frustrated being made to go through the same routine every day, doing the same paces again and again. She needed to do more exciting things with Cynthia, to have fun. Cynthia had to relax and enjoy her time with Pickle rather than pushing for more practice and more wins.

Thank you, Ponyswift89. Will try tomorrow.
TillyMagic

Suddenly, Tilly heard her mum calling
from the kitchen.

'Tilly! Hot chocolate! I've
made your favourite . . . with
marshmallows in it.'

Tilly smiled. 'For humans
only,' she said. 'Yum! I'll
come and get it!'

She slipped off her chair
and went to fetch her drink,
satisfied that tomorrow
she was going to transform Pickle and
Cynthia's relationship.

Next morning, before school, Tilly
found Cynthia in the tack room, arranging
an assortment of decorative bridles.

'Hi. How's it going?'

'Fine,' said Cynthia, in a manner that
suggested she didn't want to continue
the conversation. Tilly realised Angela

must have spoken to her about the
marshmallows, but she was determined not
to be put off.

'So do you and Pickle think you'll be
ready for the County Fair on Saturday?'
she asked brightly.

'Of course we will. Pickle was at the
famous Parkview stud, which is known for
its top quality show ponies. My mum says
she cost the Earth. I bet there aren't many
ponies that impressive round here.'

Tilly clenched her teeth. She was trying to get on with Cynthia. She really was. But when Cynthia made such snobby remarks it was hard.

'I let Pickle and Magic have some time out together yesterday,' said Tilly patiently. 'You should have seen them. They really like each other. Maybe they'll be good friends.'

'Pickle hasn't got time for friends. She's a show pony. Not a lazing around the paddock pony! I told you, if she hangs about with other horses too much she'll pick up bad habits.'

'But Magic hasn't got bad habits. He's a wonderful horse. And Pickle does need friends. Everybody does. Perhaps Pickle would perform better if you gave her the chance to relax.'

'Why should I listen to you?' said Cynthia. 'You're just being mean. You've already got me into trouble about Pickle's treats.'

'I'm sorry, Cynthia. It wasn't about

getting you in trouble. I did it for Pickle's health. You wouldn't want her being ill, would you?

'No. Of course not.'

'I watched you training with her yesterday and, well, it was obvious she wasn't enjoying it. A happy pony wouldn't keep shoving her head down with her ears back, swishing her tail and refusing to behave.'

Cynthia took a deep breath. It looked as though she was about to stamp her foot again, but instead she said, 'You ride her then. If you think you know it all, let's see how good you really are.'

Tilly was taken aback for a moment. 'Okay,' she said, taking a deep breath. 'But I think we should try something completely different. Instead of going into the sand arena, can you help me set up some bending poles in the large flat field at the bottom of the yard? We'll take some plastic hoops out there too. Pickle's going to have fun – and you're going to join in

too. I'll ask Angela if you can ride Rosie
and we'll have our very own gymkhana
race, right here at Silver Shoe!'

Cynthia looked unimpressed. 'If I
wanted to do gymkhana events I'd have
joined the Pony Club,' she grumbled.

'It might be fun,' said Tilly. 'You'll
never know unless you try. I used to hate
mushrooms, until my mum made me taste
one. Now they're my favourite. You might
feel the same way about gymkhana games.'

Cynthia shrugged. 'Well, nothing else
seems to be working, so I guess we could
give it a go.'

Forty minutes later, Tilly and Cynthia led
Pickle and Rosie down to the large field.
Tilly felt brave and nervous at the same
time. The pressure was on. She kept her
fingers crossed that her plan would work;
that she'd not only be able to help Pickle,

66

but Cynthia too.

When they reached the field, Tilly stood up straight and tried to imagine she was Angela, who always taught great lessons. She remembered the advice she'd read on the internet. She hoped it would work!

'Pickle needs to be reminded that training can be enjoyable. It's not about standing still or getting perfect paces all the time. It's about exploring and learning to get on with a rider. We're going to try a slalom course around these poles. I did it at Pony Club camp. It was great!'

'Already done it. Did it years ago,' replied Cynthia, sounding bored. 'It's babyish.'

'And it's also fun,' said Tilly defiantly. 'It's fun for Pickle.'

The girls mounted. Tilly allowed Pickle to familiarise herself with her environment, then she asked her to trot a few laps. 'Why don't you follow my lead with Rosie?' she said to Cynthia.

It was strange riding a pony again. Tilly was used to being on a big horse like Magic. It made her realise how much progress she'd made. She remembered taking her first lessons on little Bunny and Rosie, while Magic was still in training. He'd needed a lot of work because he'd never been backed before. Now, she rode him every day and people were starting to talk about what a good team they made. Champion potential, maybe? She hoped so.

Tilly used her leg to ask Pickle to canter. At first Pickle seemed reluctant, but Tilly leaned forward and whispered to her.

'Take your time. It's only a warm-up and then we're going to play some games!'

She patted her neck, then nudged with her heel again. This time Pickle responded straightaway, moving into a smooth canter. Tilly was impressed.

'Well done!' she said, rewarding Pickle with another pat.

Next, Tilly moved towards the bending poles. Pickle seemed fascinated by them, so

she allowed her to explore them with her nose. When Pickle eventually lost interest, Tilly walked her
to the end of the field.

'Okay, Pickle,' she said. 'Now we're going to weave our way in and out of these bending poles. Let's slalom!'

Pickle went forward, but instead of weaving between the poles as she was asked to, she just pushed past them. Tilly didn't mind – she knew Pickle would get it eventually. She simply laughed and got Pickle to circle and try again, but when she glanced at Cynthia, Tilly could see she had an 'I told you so' look on her face.

Several attempts later, Pickle was getting it right. She became really responsive to Tilly's aids and seemed to love every minute of the session.

'Now you have a try,' said Tilly, dismounting.

'Why did Pickle respond so well for you?' said Cynthia, pouting. 'She obviously prefers you to me.'

On Rosie, Cynthia had barely had to move. Rosie loved gymkhana games and knew exactly what she had to do.

'It's not that,' said Tilly. 'She's just enjoying the change of scenery. It's a different kind of activity so it's more exciting for her. Now, why don't we swap? I haven't ridden Rosie for ages!'

Tilly watched as Cynthia and Pickle made their way to the poles. She crossed her fingers and hoped it would work out for them. They lined themselves up and went for it. Their first go wasn't perfect and Tilly could see the frustration on Cynthia's face, but by the second and third attempts, she relaxed. She even laughed when Pickle walked straight into a pole instead of going round it. Pickle looked more relaxed too.

'Okay,' she called. 'You're right. This is fun. In fact, this is the most fun I've had with Pickle in ages!'

Then she went for her fourth go, then her fifth, then her sixth. She was lost in what she was doing and really enjoying it.

Tilly smiled to herself. She rather fancied the idea of becoming a riding instructor.

Seven

'What are you looking so pleased about, Tiger Lil?' said Tilly's dad.

Tilly had finished her homework and was sitting at the kitchen table, organising her list of 'Cynthia's Tips for the Top'.

'Do you know, I think I might like to be a riding instructor one day.'

'Really?'

'Yes. In fact, I've already started. My first ever student is the new girl, Cynthia. I helped her this morning and it went really well.'

'Good for you.'

'I suppose I'd better go and plan my next lesson with her,' said Tilly.

'Absolutely. Teachers need to plan,' said her dad, with a smile. Of course he understood. He was a maths teacher at Heathwell High in North Cosford. He was always planning and preparing lessons.

With that, Tilly put her homework away and went upstairs to work on her next session with Cynthia and Pickle.

She pulled out her magazine collection and searched for fun, bonding activities. There were all sorts of ideas, such as obstacle courses, stepping stones, and musical mats.

She decided to text Cynthia, who'd given Tilly her number after the gymkhana practice.

HI CYNTHIA. HOPE U ENJOYED UR SESSION WITH PICKLE 2DAY. WANT 2 DO IT AGAIN 2MORO? I'VE GOT LOTS OF IDEAS. T. X

A reply came straightaway.

THX TILLY. THAT WLD B GR8. X

That night, Tilly went to bed feeling proud and happy. It felt good to be giving guidance to another rider, to be sharing everything she'd learned from the team at Silver Shoe. She remembered how, when she'd first arrived at the farm, she'd seen Mia and Cally across the yard and thought how lucky they were. She'd wished she could be like them. Now they were close

friends and riding was something she did
every day. It couldn't be better.

Tilly raced to get to Silver Shoe next
morning. She was looking forward to
telling Cynthia about her ideas. Like
Tilly, Cynthia was always one of the first
to be mucking out and feeding, but while
Tilly sometimes did it in her pyjamas,
with jodhpur boots and a scruffy fleece
pulled over the top, Cynthia was always
immaculately dressed, with spotless
jodhpurs and all the latest gear.

Tilly went straight to Magic's stable.
He obviously had an itch because he was
rubbing his back legs against the stable
wall. As soon as he saw her, he pricked his
ears and came over. It was as if he'd been
waiting for her.

'Hello, handsome,' she said, stroking
his nose.

She led him outside and tied him in the yard. She could see Cynthia bobbing in and out of Pickle's stable with a pitchfork. There was no sign of marshmallows or mints, which was good.

'Morning,' she called. 'How are you?'

There was no reply.

Maybe she hadn't heard. Tilly carried on, refreshing the bedding, fetching fresh water and hay. When she had finished she went to collect Magic's grooming kit from the tack room.

As Tilly pushed open the wooden door, the smell of leather and saddle oil greeted her. She breathed it in and sighed happily. Cynthia was there, standing beside her bridle collection, removing loose hairs from Pickle's brushes with a curry comb.

'Hiya,' said Tilly.

'Hi,' said Cynthia quietly. She looked down as though she was trying to avoid catching Tilly's eye, then turned away and began straightening her bridles.

'So, are you up for another session today? I've got some time after school, if you like?'

'Um . . . maybe . . . I'm not sure . . .'

This was odd, thought Tilly. Cynthia had been so keen in her text and she'd seemed so happy after yesterday's session. Cynthia looked at the ground, then back at Tilly.

'My mum doesn't want me to,' she said awkwardly.

'Oh.'

'She doesn't think it's a good idea to interfere with Pickle's training. Not with an important show at the weekend. She

78

wants us to train the way we always do.
She says if you get involved you'll mess
everything up.'

Tilly felt crushed.

'I-I was only trying to help. I was just . . .
I've got new ideas . . . I want to . . .'

She tried to speak, to explain, but the
words came out jumbled.

'I've got to go,' said Cynthia eventually.
'I've got to get Pickle warmed up. Thanks
anyway. See you.'

'Uh, yeah . . . see you,' said Tilly.

She watched as Cynthia sloped back to the stables. Tilly could tell she was unhappy. It wasn't like her to walk so slowly. She usually marched everywhere.

Poor Pickle. She wasn't going to be keen on going back to the old regime either. It was such a shame. But it obviously wasn't Cynthia who was the problem now. It was her mum. She was the person pushing Cynthia, trying to get her to win, making her do show after show. She was the reason Pickle had such a boring training schedule and an unhealthy lifestyle.

Eight

Later that week, Brook came over to
Tilly's house for tea. He'd found a website
about the Native American tribe and their
reserve. The website wasn't finished so it
didn't say much, but it had contact details.
Brook and Tilly decided they should write
a letter. It felt like such an important step,
and sending an email seemed less personal
somehow.

They sat at the kitchen table, sharing a
plate of cookies, with Scruff at their feet.

'How do we start?' said Tilly. Her stomach was full of butterflies. She was nervous and excited at the same time. She knew there was a chance this letter could lead to them finding out more about their mum.

'Let's tell them who we are and why we're writing to them,' said Brook.

'Don't forget to tell them about the horsehair bracelets. Maybe we should send a photo of one? And I made a copy of the photo of our mum at school. Someone might recognise her.'

'You never know.'

They sat for over an hour, working on the letter and making sure each sentence was right. When it was done they showed it to Tilly's mum and dad, who both agreed it was a perfect letter. Then they carefully folded it and put it in an envelope, along with copies of the photographs, and addressed it to the tribe chief, whose name had been on the website.

'Done,' said Brook. 'Let's go and post it.'

They walked through the quiet main
street of the village, taking turns to hold
the letter.

'It's so exciting,' said Tilly. 'It feels like
the start of something really amazing.'

'We'll see,' said Brook. 'They might
not reply of course. Or they might not
think there's any connection between
our horsehair bracelets and theirs. But it's
worth a try. Fingers crossed, eh?'

'Fingers crossed.'

Together they lifted the little white
envelope to the mouth of the post-box.

'Ready?'

'One . . . two . . . three . . .'

The envelope slipped from their fingers and clattered to the bottom.

'It's got a long journey ahead of it.'

'Let's hope it's a good one.'

Tilly and Brook looked at each other, smiled, and then hugged. In that moment, Tilly knew it didn't matter whether anything came from the letter or not. The most important thing was that she had Brook and he had her. She could tell he was thinking the same.

'Right, I'd better get back to Cavendish Hall,' said Brook. 'I've got to give Solo

a decent groom. I'm taking him to the
Cosford County Fair at the weekend. By
the way, how's your work with Cynthia
and Pickle going?'

'Oh, it started really well but . . . they
didn't want my help in the end,' said Tilly,
her voice low. 'They're doing it their way.'

'That's a shame,' said Brook, giving
Tilly's arm a squeeze. 'Their loss though.'

After Brook had gone, Tilly's dad drove her
to Silver Shoe. Tilly was quiet. Although
she was happy about the letter, the
Cynthia/Pickle problem was still bothering
her. Her dad kept glancing over at her to
check she was okay.

'Call me when you want a pick up,' he
said, pulling into the lane. 'And . . . cheer
up!'

'I'm okay.'

'Sure? I can always tell when there's

something on your mind, Tiger Lil'. Tell
me about it.'

Tilly stared down at her boots and
gathered her thoughts.

'Do you remember when I said one
day I'd like to become a riding instructor?
I thought I'd be good at it. But now . . .
I don't know if I've got what it takes.'

'Of course you have, Tiger Lil'.
Everyone always says you've got a gift with
horses. Why would you think you're not up
to it?'

'It's not the horses, Dad. It's the
people. They don't want my help. They
think I'll mess things up for them.'

'Well, they obviously don't know how
talented you are. You've helped lots of
horses at Silver Shoe. Remember how
you helped Angela get over her nerves
and compete with Pride and Joy? That
was fantastic! You'll find a way of proving
yourself. I know you!'

Tilly smiled. Her dad's faith in her
made her feel a lot better. She looked over

at the gates of Silver Shoe and felt a sparkle
of excitement again. She thought of Magic,
waiting for her. At least he always wanted
her around.

'Bye, Dad,' she said, kissing his cheek.
'And thanks.'

As Tilly walked through the five-bar
gate, she could see Angela in the yard,
talking to the farrier, Stephen. It was a
pleasant September evening, still warm
but with a hint of autumn breeze.

'Hi, Tilly.' Angela waved her over.
'If you've got a minute, could you do me
a quick favour? Tell Duncan that Stephen
is here. He's over at the sand school, with
Cynthia and Pickle.'

'Sure.'

Tilly took a shortcut, between the
stable blocks, and found Duncan standing
at the fence, looking very frustrated,
while Cynthia was struggling with Pickle.
Cynthia's mum was at the opposite fence,
shouting instructions to her daughter. It
was clear she wasn't helping the situation.

'Stephen's here,' said Tilly. 'He's in the yard.'

'Hooray!' whispered Duncan. 'You've saved Pickle. I'll take her up. I told Cynthia's mum I didn't think it was a good idea to keep training so hard. But obviously she's decided that she's going to oversee all Pickle's training from now on. She's more of a hindrance than a help. The words 'control freak' spring to mind! She takes everything so seriously.'

'At least Pickle's weight seems to be going in the right direction,' Tilly said. 'That's good.'

From the fence, she could see Pickle had lost a bit of weight. Her body looked lighter, and in better proportion with her dainty head.

'Yes, thankfully Cynthia seems to be getting the message,' said Duncan. 'She's cut out all the unnecessary treats. She's trying her best. I just hope her mum does too. I saw a bag of fudge in her hand earlier. She was waving it temptingly at Pickle and when Cynthia told her not to, she said: "I'll decide whether Pickle gets treats or not!"'

Tilly shook her head. Now she felt sorry for Pickle and Cynthia. At least she knew she'd managed to give them some help.

Tilly spent the rest of the evening in the paddock with Magic. She wasn't in the mood for riding. She just wanted to chat to him. She always found it helpful to tell him what was on her mind. He stood happily grazing, occasionally looking up to check she was still nearby.

'So, the good news is, Brook and I have sent a letter to the Native American tribe. Let's see if we get a reply.'

Magic lifted his head.

'But the bad news is that your friend Pickle is going through show pony training hell! Oh, Magic, I tried to help. I really did. But what can I do if they don't want it? They've got the Cosford County Fair in a few days. It's going to be embarrassing for Cynthia if Pickle doesn't cooperate in front of the judges, but the way things are going, she's in no mood to perform to order.'

Nine

On the day of the Cosford County Fair, the sky clouded over. By midday, it was heavy and grey and looked ready to rain at any moment. The rain didn't bother Tilly. She was happy to ride in any weather, as long as the horses didn't mind. She wasn't so sure how Cynthia and Pickle would cope though.

Tilly arrived at the fair with her family. There was so much to see and do, it was hard to agree where to go first.

'I think I'll check out the field sports,'

said Tilly's dad. 'There's a demonstration on fly fishing. Are you coming, Adam?'

'Yeah, but also I want to see the birds of prey. And the massive tractors. And the quad bikes. And the . . .'

'What about the craft tent?' said Mrs Redbrow. 'That's what I want to look at.'

'Boring!' said Adam.

'Why don't we do our own thing then arrange a meeting time?' said Tilly.

'Good idea.'

'How about three-thirty, by the horse and hound arena? Then we can watch the

show ponies. '

'Perfect.'

'What will you do now, Tilly? Fancy looking at the craft tent with me?' said Tilly's mum.

'Er, no thanks,' Tilly replied. She knew exactly what she was going to do. She'd just spotted Mia and Cally in the crowd. 'I'll see you later,' she said, running to catch up with her friends.

'Definitely a day for Wellies,' said Cally, as they trudged over the muddy grass.

Despite the bad weather, the showground was crammed with visitors. They passed a large covered tent where local farmers were selling jam and cheese, then made their way over to the Cavendish Hall trailer. Brook was standing outside with Solo, sharing jumping tips with one of his friends.

'Hi,' he said, as they approached.

'Solo's looking great,' said Cally. 'What time are you on?'

'Not until the end of the day. What time is that spoilt pony, Pickle, doing her show class?'

'It's not Pickle who's spoilt,' said Tilly defensively.

'It's Cynthia,' said Mia.

'It's not even Cynthia,' said Tilly. 'If you ask me, it's her mum.'

'I guess we'll see how they get on today,' said Cally.

Suddenly there was a commotion from the horsebox that had just pulled in behind them. It was the sound of arguing.

'I know those voices,' said Tilly.

'And I recognise that super-flash horsebox,' said Mia.

The four friends watched as Cynthia and her mum stomped out, one behind the other. Cynthia's face was red and she looked upset.

'I'm NOT wearing those stupid boots!' she shouted. 'I want my old boots. My lucky boots.'

Cynthia's mum was waving a box of brand new jodhpur boots at her.

'These ones will be lucky too!' she said.

'No. They won't!'

'Well, they're the latest version. I had to order them from Germany. None of the other girls will have boots as good as this.

Do you want to look like a winner or not?'

'It doesn't matter what I look like, does it?' snapped Cynthia. 'Thanks to you, Pickle and I are going to lose!'

'What have I done? All I've done is try to help you.'

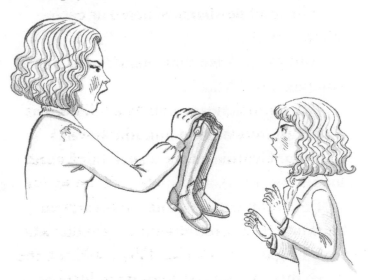

'You wouldn't let us train the way we wanted to. If you'd let us have a bit of fun, Pickle would behave herself.'

'Don't be silly. The reason Pickle doesn't behave is because you're not firm enough with her. I've told you a thousand times, you have to be firmer with the leg.'

'But Tilly said . . .'

'Oh! Don't start that again! Tilly. Tilly. Tilly. What does Tilly know? Has she ever done five horse shows in seven days, up and down the country? No. Didn't think so.'

Tilly and her friends stared at each other.

'Mmm . . . I see your point,' said Brook thoughtfully.

Tilly, Brook, Cally and Mia followed as Pickle was led to the competition warm-up arena. Cynthia glanced back briefly and gave Tilly an anxious, apologetic smile, but other than that, she and her mum argued the whole way, even disagreeing about who was going to lead Pickle. Tilly could see the angry shouting was bothering the little pony.

'She's definitely not going to be in a mood to show if they keep that up,' she said.

'It's a pity,' said Cally, 'because she looks like a perfect show pony. Everything about her is in proportion.'

'It is now,' said Tilly.

'Should we try to stop them arguing?' asked Mia.

Tilly had an idea.

She marched towards Cynthia and her mum and gave a little cough. They both turned sharply. Pickle neighed, as though she was welcoming her.

'Oh, hello there, Tilly,' said Cynthia's mum, in a fake-friendly way.

'Hi. I just wanted to give Cynthia this.'

She handed Cynthia a small strip of twisted horsehair.

'It's a bracelet made from Pickle's tail hairs. I made it when I groomed her the other day. I thought you'd like it before

you go in front of the judges. It will bring you luck.'

'Thanks,' said Cynthia. She took the bracelet, then she stared at Tilly. 'That's so nice of you.'

Cynthia's mum didn't say anything.

'Is your class soon?' Tilly asked, as she stroked Pickle's nose. She could sense her agitation. She hoped the stroking would soothe her.

'Any minute,' said Cynthia. 'But . . . oh . . .'

She took a deep breath. Her eyes filled with tears. 'I don't think I want to now.'

She looked at Tilly then at her mum.

'I – I've had enough. I don't want to go into the ring today. All week my training has been a disaster and I just don't think I can do it.'

'What?'

Cynthia's mum's eyes bulged. She looked as though she was about to explode.

'I want Tilly to ride Pickle today,' said Cynthia shakily. 'Would you do that, Tilly?

She likes you so much and the way you handled her . . .'

Cynthia's mum frowned.

Tilly shrugged. 'Er . . .'

'Please? You'll bring out the best in her. Pickle looks so good now she's lost weight. I want to give her the chance to impress the judges and you're the one who can make that happen. Not me.'

Tilly tried to back away. Cynthia and her mum had enough problems without her getting involved. But Cynthia was determined.

'Please?'

She held Pickle's reins out to Tilly. Tilly wasn't sure, but then she caught Pickle's eye. There was a strange, hopeful look on her face. Suddenly it felt as though there was no one in the world except the two of them. Tilly held out her hand and let Pickle caress it. In that moment, she knew. She had to do it. For Cynthia. For Pickle.

Ten

There was no time to think. Tilly had
watched Cynthia and Pickle practise so
many times, she was sure she'd remember
what to do. She was already wearing
jodhpurs and riding boots, so she just
needed to borrow Cynthia's navy blue jacket
and helmet. The jacket was a bit tight and
she didn't look as smart as the other riders,
but this was Pickle's show, not hers.

'Good luck, Tilly,' said Cynthia, as she
dabbed her red eyes with a tissue.

Cynthia's mum kept her cross expression, but did manage to offer a few supportive words.

'Well, I hope you do manage to get the best from Pickle. I want her to have her chance in front of the judges. She's cost me a lot of money.'

Once Tilly had mounted, she and Pickle spent ten minutes going round the outside of the ring in walk, trot and canter with the other ponies and their riders. Then the judges pulled everyone into the centre of the ring, where they all lined up, ready to do their individual shows. When Pickle's number was called, Tilly walked out of the line-up. Pickle looked round and gave a little nod, as if she was letting Tilly know she was glad to have her in charge.

'It's okay, girl. You've got me today. Just do your stuff, like you've been practising. Let's show those judges how beautifully you move. Prick your ears and show off your paces today, then I promise I'll make sure you get to have more fun with your training

in future. As long as you're at Silver Shoe,
I'll look out for you. And Magic. He'll be
looking out for you too.'

Pickle stood very still, and Tilly could
sense she was ready to cooperate. Tilly
smiled at the judges. She hoped they
wouldn't spot the too-small jacket and
unpolished boots. With any luck Pickle
would dazzle them so much that they
wouldn't notice.

'Okay, here we go,' whispered Tilly.
'It's your chance to shine, Parkview Pickle!
Remember your manners. Be as elegant
as you can. And above all, please behave
yourself.'

Pickle straightened up. She was
wearing a top-of-the-range showing saddle
and a delicate sparkly snaffle bridle, which
showed off her pretty face. She looked
great, even if Tilly didn't.

They worked through the paces again,
from a walk to a trot to a canter. With each
figure of eight, Pickle seemed to get better
and better. She was supple and balanced.

There was no sign of the naughty pony who'd misbehaved in the arena at Silver Shoe.

'That's it, girl! You show 'em!' said Tilly, rewarding Pickle with encouragement on the final gallop.

They finished in front of the judges, coming to a neat halt, and stood for a while, so the judges could see how well-mannered Pickle was. Tilly saw Cynthia and her mum in the crowd. Cynthia was smiling. And although Cynthia's mum still looked stern, there was the trace of a smile on her lips too.

The judges nodded and signalled they were finished.

As Tilly and Pickle went back to the line, Cynthia entered the ring with a grooming box. Together, they removed Pickle's saddle, and Cynthia gave her a quick wipe with a stable rubber, before the next part of the show.

Now the judges would inspect Pickle's conformation and watch them walk and trot in hand. Tilly was pleased to be third in line so that she could see how the first two ponies were trotted up. When every pony had done its individual show and conformation, they all went around the ring together again. Then, tense with anticipation, Tilly, Pickle, and the other ponies and riders, waited for the judges to announce their winner.

Tilly thought the decision seemed to take forever. Finally, a gentleman wearing a bowler hat signalled to her to come forward into the centre of the ring. Was this another test she didn't know about? It wasn't until Tilly heard the cheers from the crowd that she realised – Pickle had won the class!

In the lap of honour, Tilly caught sight of Mia, Cally and Brook. They were standing at the fence, waving their hands, and shouting, 'Well done!'

Tilly gave them a cheeky grin and waved back.

'You were fab!' said Cynthia, smiling as Tilly dismounted. 'And so were you, Pickle!'

They gathered at the edge of the fence. Cynthia curled an arm round Pickle's shoulder and smothered her with kisses. It was great to see her reward Pickle with love rather than sugar, thought Tilly, as she watched Pickle nuzzle Cynthia's cheek.

'I suppose I need to thank you, Tilly,' said Cynthia's mum. 'You obviously do have a knack for getting the best out of a horse. If only you could teach some of that to Cynthia.'

'I think Cynthia will do fine,' said Tilly.

She smiled at Cynthia and winked. Cynthia winked back then stroked Pickle's nose. Moments later, Brook, Mia and Cally emerged from the crowds, closely followed by the Redbrows.

'You didn't tell us you were riding today, Tiger Lil',' said Tilly's dad.

'You didn't even tell us!' Mia exclaimed. 'And we were only with you five minutes before.'

'Um . . . it was a last minute thing,' said Tilly. 'I was doing Cynthia a favour.'

'You looked good,' said Brook. 'The riding hat was a bit wonky, but the paces were smooth!'

'Perfection isn't everything,' said Tilly. 'Pickle enjoyed it, that's the main thing.'

'Absolutely!' said Cynthia, and with that

she gave Pickle another kiss.

Tilly was glad. It seemed as if Cynthia and Pickle were going to be happy from now on. She couldn't help feeling proud that she'd been the one who'd helped make it happen. And she looked forward to doing a lot more with them in the future.

'Hey, Tiger Lil',' said her dad.

'Still not sure about becoming a riding instructor?'

Tilly gave him a knowing smile, then she caught Pickle's eye.

'Do you think I'd make a good riding instructor?'

Pickle snorted. Everyone laughed. And Tilly felt on top of the world.

Pippa's Top Tips

Always act responsibly around the yard – make sure you leave things safe and tidy and that your tack is cleaned properly.

When riding on the roads, stay aware at all times. Be on the look out for anything that might spook your pony.

Don't be afraid to use hand signals to slow the traffic down, then nod your head or raise your hand to say thank you.

If a large lorry comes along, make the driver wait, if you can, then trot to the nearest gateway or driveway so he can pass.

Always pay attention to your pony's behaviour – it's the only way they can communicate their feelings.

Remember, no amount of training will make a horse successful if their owner doesn't understand their needs.

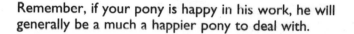

Too much training can be counter-productive. Take time to have fun with your pony too.

Remember, if your pony is happy in his work, he will generally be a much a happier pony to deal with.

Over-feeding is all too common a problem. Indulging your pony will make him overweight and unhealthy, putting pressure on his limbs, and more fat around his vital organs.

Reward your horse or pony with love and affection, rather than sweet treats or extra food. There's nothing wrong with the odd polo or carrot, as long as your pony doesn't come to expect them!

For more about Tilly and Silver Shoe Farm –
including pony tips, quizzes and everything
you ever wanted to know about horses –
visit www.tillysponytails.co.uk